Teacher's I

FREE BOOK HAPPY READING
This Book is NOT For Resale
Donations of Books/Mags/Comics
In ANY Condition Are Welcome!
Please Return Me & Thank You!

Copyright © 2024 S.J James All rights reserved

ISBN: 9798340095817

The characters and events portrayed in this book are fictitious. Any similarity to real persons, living or dead, is coincidental and not intended by the author.

No part of this book may be reproduced, or stored in a retrieval system, or transmitted in any form or by any means, electronic, mechanical, photocopying, recording, or otherwise, without express written permission of the publisher.

Preface

This story contains themes of child abuse. Discretion advised.

Happy was I the day word broke out- "teacher's dead."

Happy was I as the news anchor repeated herself, and Mum grabbed the back of the dining chair in shock.

Happy was I to read the words on Dad's paper even as he threw it down to catch Mum as she collapsed- 'Local School Teacher Found Dead.

27-year-old Katherine Darling was found in the marshes last night…'

Happy was I to imagine her struggling in her last moments, perhaps even begging for mercy, confused at how quickly things had unravelled.
I stared down at my dragon cake, red velvet and blue frosting, ten glittering candles decorating it's border.

Happy was I that day, but I didn't smile. I couldn't.

Instead I blew out the candles.

***

Happy was I on the eve before my 9th birthday. Mum promised to take me to get my ears pierced and I'd get to pick out my own earrings in the store.

Happy was I to learn we were going to 'BL(INK)'S' tattoo shop behind the corner shop across from school. Principal Richards always warned the older kids not to hang around the chicken shop afterschool, as it was a few doors down the tattoo place, which always had men outside smoking and licking sheets of what looked to be tracing paper , while others fought over wood glue and deodorant cans.

Happy was I when Mum started working earlier at the GP, and Dad started to take me to school. Mum

always made me walk of the opposite side of him whenever we walked past so that I couldn't see what they were doing, but Dad would let me wave and ask about their buzzed hair, and piercings all over their face.
I liked the guy with metal spikes on his head, Rufie, who actually worked at the shop. Everyday he changed the colours of the studs and it made him look like a – "rainbow hedgehog dementor!"- which he found funny, even as Dad tugged me away with a - "Kids huh?"

Happy was I when he offered to pierce my ears in a few years –"If your parents say yes."

Happy was I when I asked Mum about piercing my ears and Dad took my side –"It's a pretty decent spot, they look bad but they're pretty decent, once you get past the purple horns," – and Mum finally agreed.

Happy was I when Mum called me down that morning, saying she had a surprise. I raced down, thinking I was getting a birthday party, only to see a blond lady by the door, wearing a light blue cardigan and a spotted dress by the door. She had a box in her hands that seemed to vibrate on its own; when Mum offered to put it on the table for her, she opened it to show me the hamster inside. It looked terrified, and kept running around the box, bumping into the sides and mouthing at edges of the box.

Happy was I when Mum took the box away. I don't like small animals, unless they move slowly, or have lots of legs, like my cousin's tarantula.

Happy was I when Mum asked me to bring the tea tray. Katherine- "Call me Kittie," – smiled a lot, and she blinked a lot more than normal. Or maybe she blinked normally, and because of her large eyes, it felt like she blinked too much. She used to be my babysitter, when I was one or two –"Gosh, you've grown up, haven't you!"- and was back in town for her new job at my school. She hoped I liked my gift.

Happy was I when Mum said I could go to my room, but that feeling quickly left when it became clear she was coming too. Mum thought we could catch up, and –"Maybe Kittie could take you to Claire's to get your ears done! They have such a nice collection-".

Happy was I when Mum left the door open, although I didn't know why. Kittie seemed nice enough, she spoke about Leeds, Glascow and Manchester, about accents and sheep in roads, all the while touching my books and peering at my stone collection on my desk. I couldn't decide which I wanted more, for her to leave, or for her to stop talking. She moved my Spiderwick books off my desk and suggested we get a cage for- "Harry, or Henry- there aren't *that* many H names, now that I think about it,"- and I hummed in response. *Its* name was Mordor, and it was going to stay in the bathroom so I wouldn't have to hear it running around.

Happy was I when Mum announced it was time to go- until I realised she really meant for Kittie to take me. To *Claire's*. I was livid, and made sure to bang the door so that the antique knocker clanged against the door. It belonged to Mum's aunt Eden or something, so Mum always makes a fuss if we close the door too hard. Sure enough, I could hear her muffled yell as we headed down towards the bus stop. Suddenly she grabbed my arm, and I tried not to flinch. She looked around and whispered "Do you still want to go to BL(INK)'S?"

Happy was I even as I screamed, while Rufie and his blue haired friend laughed and gave me a high five – "Ya' got lungs of steel on ya', Shortcake-", and let me hold Pidgin, the stick insect shop mascot as a reward.

Happy was I on the way home, so happy I even gave Kittie a hug in thanks when we got home. Mum was happy to see us bond, and decided against a tirade about the doorknocker, especially when Kittie mentioned she'd forgotten about the door and accidentally closed it too hard. We said our goodbyes and later that evening, high on salted caramel frosting, I brought Mordor in to sleep by my bed, on my desk, *next* to my Spiderwick Chronicles.

Happy was I when school started back after the half term and Kittie

turned out to be my new Science teacher.
During break times, I helped her set up experiments for the next class, and lunchtimes were spent scarfing down hummus, carrot and cucumber pittas and half bruised apples, before racing down to her classroom to talk about what makes diamonds, and where to find the most gemstones based on geography.

Happy was I when Mum offered to have her babysit me unofficially for the weekend so they could go to visit Dad's sister, Aunt Enas, who had broken her leg falling down the stairs on a bus a week before moving into her new flat. It sounded like the best weekend ever- Kittie offered to take us to the marshes to see if we could spot some jade or tiger's eye and agate stones, and Mum had arranged for me to go to my friend Sophie's for a sleepover if there were any problems.

Happy was I when we found an amethyst and lots of coloured quartz on our trip. I wore my Mum's wellies with Dad's waterproof's on top, and Kittie wore a zebra striped jumpsuit with silver wellies. It made for a funny picture, us covered in mud and grass.

Happy was I when Kittie offered to put the stones in a rock tumbler she had back at her flat.
She lived on the other side of school, and as we walked past BL(INK)'S, Rufie was by the window, a balloon in his mouth as he bent over

someone's arm with a tattoo gun. He stopped and waved as he caught sight of us, and I remember his spikes were neon green with pink tips that day.

Happy was I when we got to Kittie's flat- it was on the fifth floor, and the lift was broken. By the time we got to the door, we were wheezing and laughing so hard, she had tears on her face, and I kept snorting. Mum would've had a fit if she'd seen me then.

Happy was I when Kittie offered to get us a change of clothes and a warm shower. She led me to the bathroom and, still snorting, I told her I was old enough to wash by myself now that I was nine. She laughed and left the door open on her way out.

Happy was I, still giggling as I got out of the tub ten minutes later, only to find Kittie in the doorway, a towel in her hand. For a while nothing was said. Then I giggled nervously and made for the towel. Kittie smiled at me- "You're growing into quite the young lady,"- and handed me a large t-shirt that, once I quickly pulled it on, reached my shins.
"My turn," she said, before taking off her t-shirt and heading for the shower. I averted my eyes and headed for the living room, where she'd lain out the rocks we'd found, as well as the tumbling kit.

Happy was I in that moment, the sound of Oggy and the Cockroaches in the background – "Zee ze zee ze zee ze zay zay zee zee zee zee zeee…"- that I didn't notice the shower had stopped.

I jumped when I felt Kittie's hand on my shoulder, and turned to her with a nervous smile. She handed me a glass of orange juice, and I gulped it down nervously ass her owlish eyes blinked at me. Once. Twice. Again. Thrice.

Happy was I when she finally turned her gaze to the table and began talking, about fine grit, and silicon carbide, polish and tumbling. Tumbling. That was the last word I remembered, over and over again.

Tumbling.

Tumbling.

Tumbling.

Tumbling.

Tumbling.

Tumbling. Tumbling.
Tumbling.Tumbling. Tumbling.
Tumbling.Tumbling.TumblingTumb
lingTumblingTumblingTumblingTu
mblingTumblingTumblingTumbling
TumblingTumblingTumblingTumbli
ngTumblingTumblingTumblingTum
blingTumblingTumblingTumblingTu
mblingTumblingTumblingTumbling
TumblingTumblingTumblingTumbli
ngTumblingTumblingTumblingTum
blingTumblingTumblingTumblingTu
mblingTumblingTumblingTumbling
TumblingTumblingTumblingTumbli
ngTumblingTumblingTumblingTum
blingTumblingTumblingTumblingTu

mblingTumblingTumblingTumblingt
umblingtumblingtumblingtumblingt
umblingtumbling
tumbllingtumbellingtumbling,
tumblin-

Happy was I when I woke up with
no memory.
I was happy because I had been
dreaming about Byron the Griffin,
and how Simon takes such good care
of him. I had been flying on Byron's
back before I came tumbling back to
bed, and onto the floor. Cool hands
helped me up, and I looked up into
Kittie's eyes. They had always
seemed big, but now they seemed to
eat up half her face. Like Dobby. Or
Gollum. I tried to imaging Gollum in
a light blue sweater and polka dot

dress squealing, "My preciousss," only to trip over his skirt.

Happy was I with that image in mind, that the journey home remains a blur of steps, street lights flickering on as the skies darkened, and neon green spikes with pink tips flashing by from a car window.

Happy was I to fall back onto Byron's saddle as in the real world, my body hurt and my legs wouldn't work properly. I itched and burned all over, but I couldn't say where or why because my head felt full of cotton wool. Or cotton candy.

Happy was I when I woke up to Mum's warm hands cradling my face, Dad's anxious face in the background - "Is it a flu? I've never seen her like this,"- and Gollum's blond hair tickling my nose.

Happy was I to miss a week of school. Mum and Dad had stayed home to check on me, and I spent my days in bed knowing something was very wrong, but not knowing *what*.

Happy was I when Mum and Dad walked me to school the next week. I skipped between them before spotting Rufie by the door of the tattoo shop. He seemed to be arguing with Mr Blue and another man I'd seen before, a giant man with black sections on his arms, like in year one, when Jaden Barker had drawn sharpie all over my hand, and Mum had thrown a fit and called his parents. Suddenly, Rufie spotted us heading down and stuck his head of the shop to wave at me.

Happy was I to wave back, even as Mum tightened her hold on my other hand. He was saying something that seemed to relieve him- "Haven't seen you in a while, Shortcake, you didn't seem too good last Saturday-" - but I was focused on his head. His spikes were gone, and his head looked awfully bare without them.

Happy was I when he gave me a high five and promised the spikes would be back the next day. Happier was I to learn that Kittie wasn't at school either. Something about the last week made my stomach twist uncomfortably. Mordor was back in the bathroom.

Happy was I when things started to get back to normal. Dad walked me to school, Rufie's hair was spikier than ever, and the first day Kittie returned, she brought a few gemstones from the collection to show me how they were going. When she invited me to see how the rest were doing, I agreed, and after a phone call, I was back at her flat. She brought me a glass of orange juice, but I could only get through a few gulps before I felt the urge to vomit. And then I did, and the sight of orange tumbling against the hardwood floor made my head hurt.

Happy was I when I woke up an hour later, not having realised I fell asleep. As Kittie walked me home, I realised that funny felling was back, only this time, it felt stronger than before. We approached BL(INK)'S, and I felt strangely safe, knowing I'd see Rufie's head poking out at any moment.

Happy was I when it did, in full turquoise glory, and he intercepted us, crossing the street at a jog. He spoke with Kittie for a bit- "Hey, I remember you, right? The babysitter? Oh teacher, nice-"- before crouching to give me a fist bump. I missed his hand entirely, which made us all laugh, only his eyes weren't laughing as they lingered on mine. The normal swamp green was hard and glinted like polished jade as my own black eyes reflected back at me.

Kittie gave a pointed cough, and Rufie let us go with a tight smile.

Happy was I when Mum mentioned she wasn't entirely comfortable with all the time Kittie spent with me both in and out of school. We were eating dinner, I was trying to figure out why my sausages kept rolling away from my spoon, and distantly I heard Mum mention a playdate. I perked up at the thought, but my sausages went tumbling onto the floor.

Happy was I to see my friend Sophie that weekend, and we spent the day creating mazes and obstacle courses for Mordor. She loved him. I wanted to see if he'd sink or swim in the pool. He sank. Sophie fished him out before he had a chance to drown, but Mum still looked on, concerned.

Happy was I when I learned I'd be going home with Sophie and for the week. We left with Sophie's older sister- "Jessi, with an I"- who, at 15, was old enough to walk us from school to our street. She stopped by the chicken shop to say hi to some of her friends, and Sophie's little brother Luca seized that distraction and tugged her hair. As she turned to yell at him, I felt a light tug on my own.

Happy was I to see Rufie smiling down at me. He showed me a new set of spikes he just had delivered, scaled, to look like the barbs on a dragon's tale. As Sophie and Luca caught sight of the spikes and peered up at them, Rufie took me aside, and after a glance around, he crouched down again and asked me a small question. A question that I had been asking myself.

Happy was I when I answered him, and he straightened with a nod. After another high five, he was back across the street, and we were heading home to Sophie's. Every day that week, he'd come up to me, show off his new spikes, crouch down and ask me another question. I'd respond with a word, then two, a phrase, then a confession, until by the end, he'd collected enough of the puzzle to let me go.

In class, Kittie smiled at me, and showed me her latest collection- "-can't wait to tumble them, make them shiny and new-" -I gave a tight smile and skipped out with Sophie.

Happy was I when running around outside during lunch, and swapping pesto pasta salad for turkey bacon rashers, my orange juice remained untouched.

She pulled me aside as school ended and the class filed out, asking "Would you like me to walk you home?"

Happy was I to tell her no.

Happy was I to learn years later that Rufus knew more than he let on, more than even I knew at the time.

Happy was I that he knew the signs, and how to intervene.

He also knew a couple of friends who were handy with a lockpick.

Happy was I the day I woke up for school and heard about her disappearance.

Happier was I the day she was found.

Epilogue

It all spilled out on the parlour bench, years later, 90 minutes at a time. As needles drilled into me, the now familiar buzzing drowning the bites of pain.

"Did you know it was my birthday?" I asked the spiked porcupine bent over my leg in quiet concentration.

"I do believe ya' mentioned it when ya' walked in," he chuckled.

"No," I snorted. "I meant- that day."

Rufie paused for a moment and glanced up at me. "No, I didn't, but funny how things work out, isn't it?"

With that, he passed the cloth over my calf, revealing the words I'd practiced over and over in the councillor's room on my path to healing, as my parents tearfully looked on from the mirror.

Happy was I.

Also by S.J James

The Incoming Cycle

A small town is shaken after the gruesome death of twelve-year-old Harrison Lane. The suspects- his four closest friends. No one believes them when they blame it on the monsters, yet as strange happenings follow them to their new homes, they are forced to confront the truth, else risk destroying everyone around them.

Incoming.

Richard Keanes has only his mother and his friends in his life. Yet when a seemingly freak occurrence costs him everything and everyone he cares about, he is forced to face the aftermath alone- and the end is only the beginning.

Incoming: Road Runner *

Matthieu Walburgess had everything- until That Night. Sent to Father John's Guided Academy, a Catholic reformation school, Matthieu tries to make the most of what he's left with, while shadows from his past appear, determined to destroy his one chance at redemption.

Incoming: Red Light*

Dennis St. Louis was already on his second chance when the monsters appeared. Now he's in a country he barely remembers, with a man he's never met and an impending sense of dread. While everyone tries to forget, Dennis is plagued by the memories, which he seems to remember clearer than anyone else. When tragedy strikes again, Dennis risks it all to make things right.

Incoming: Shadows of a Lion's Claw *

Xzalia Naidoo has lived by the tales of her warrior ancestors her entire life, determined to follow in their footsteps. As Commander, she was labelled the mastermind in a night of horrors she was unable to prevent and is taken back to her homeland, where she learns the truth of what it means to be a leader- when things go wrong, it's you who pays the ultimate price.

*eBook available for pre-order on Amazon

Liked this book? Leave a review!

Printed in Great Britain
by Amazon